The Maiden Poodle

Poodle

(A Fairy Tail)

Also by S.G. Browne

NOVELS

Less Than Hero

Big Egos

Lucky Bastard

Fated

Breathers

NOVELLAS

I Saw Zombies Eating Santa Claus

SHORT STORY COLLECTIONS

Shooting Monkeys in a Barrel

SHORT STORY SINGLES

Dr. Sinister's Home for Retired Villains

Remedial English for Reanimated Corpses

Scattered Showers with a Chance of Daikaiju

The Maiden Poodle

(A Fairy Tail)

S. G. Browne

This book is a work of fiction. Any references to real dogs, real cats, or real places are used fictitiously or are the products of the author's imagination. Any resemblance to actual places or animals, living or dead, is purely coincidental. No animals were harmed in the writing of this fairy tail.

Cover design by Byron Buslig

ISBN 978-1-5214-2860-3

For Diane

Introduction

For those of you who have read any of my previous books, it would be understandable for you to expect this story to be a supernatural dark comedy about an unmarried poodle during the time of King Arthur, with some social satire throw in for good measure.

The Maiden Poodle is not one of those books.

While there is a fair amount of humor involved, it's on the lighter and more playful side. And although I've incorporated a hint of fantasy and the supernatural into the story, you won't find any immortal personifications of fate or any designer drugs that allow you to become Elvis Presley. You also won't find any super heroes, luck poachers, or zombies.

Here there be poodles.

But not just poodles. There also be Scotties, Saint Bernards, border collies, golden retrievers, beagles, greyhounds, German shepherds, and numerous other dog breeds—all of them of the anthropomorphic variety and living together in the ancient kingdom of Felinia.

Oh yes. And cats. Did I mention there were cats?

Tortoiseshells, Persians, and tabbies. Himalayans, Russian blues, and orange flame points. Black cats, white cats, and rare Norwegian forest cats.

I've been a cat person ever since I was a small child, as we always had a cat or two as part of the family. That's the way I think of my cats: as family members rather than family pets. For most of my adult life I've been the parent of at least one four-legged feline, and over the past twenty or so years that number has fluctuated between one and five. As far as I'm concerned, a cat's purr is like a salve for the soul.

And while we had dogs around while I was growing up, it wasn't until later in life when I learned to appreciate the unique qualities that dogs bring to the table. There's nothing like the pure, unabashed joy of several dogs chasing each other around a park. And when a dog smiles and wags its tail, you can't help but catch his (or her) contagious happiness.

The title character in *The Maiden Poodle* is named after the black standard poodle who captured my heart and turned me into a dog person. In addition, several other dogs and more than half a dozen cats who appear as characters in this story are inspired by and named after dogs and cats I've had the pleasure of knowing at one point or another. So in a way, *The Maiden Poodle* is a love letter to the cats and dogs who have enriched my life over the years and to dogs and cats everywhere. While I like to think of it as a fairy tale for the animal loving child in every adult, it's also suitable for children who love dogs and cats.

I hope you enjoy reading it as much as I enjoyed writing it.

The Maiden Poodle

Poodle

(A Fairy Tail)

Chapter 1

Once upon a time, in a faraway land secluded by towering cliffs and The Great Sea, existed the ancient kingdom of Felinia.

Felinia was a beautiful land, filled with fields of purple heather and natural gardens of roses and irises and tulips that captured every color of the rainbow. And throughout Felinia, ancient redwoods grew among great sprawling oaks and majestic maples—the leaves of which burned each October with the colors of autumn.

The inhabitants of Felinia were felines and canines of all breeds—the cats, naturally, filling the role of nobility, while the dogs led simple lives as peasants and farmers. It was a comfortable arrangement enjoyed by all, taken advantage of by none, with both the nobles and the peasants co-existing peacefully for generations.

However, after the passing of the Queen of Felinia, the regal Lilith the Just, the rule of the kingdom fell into the paws of her eldest heir: the despot and self-proclaimed King Griffen the Great.

Under King Griffen's rule, Felinia became a land divided between the nobles and the peasants, the rich and the poor. Soon after King Griffen took the throne, the land that had belonged to the peasants was given to the barons— the peasants turned into servants and forced to work the land for dirty water and stale dog biscuits.

Out of the poor conditions that had fallen upon the canines, an uprising took seed and began to root, swiftly turning into a call to arms, a call for a revolution. Upon hearing of this revolt, King Griffen sent his guards into the village, where more than two-dozen terriers, retrievers, hounds, spaniels, shepherds, and every dog suspected of treason was arrested and thrown into the castle dungeon.

Among those captured was a foreigner, a black standard poodle named Camille, who hailed from the enchanted land of Watonia and who was rumored to possess mystical powers that could help deliver the canines from the claws of the evil King Griffen. But with the Maiden Poodle locked up in the castle dungeon, the peasants of Felinia gave up their hope of a revolution and resigned themselves to a life of despair.

This is where our story begins.

Chapter 2

Early one morning, with the dawn slowly creeping across Felinia, a greyhound in a dark cape raced through the empty streets, hiding in shadows and darting across alleyways. Upon reaching the back entrance of a blacksmith's, the greyhound rapped softly on the door three times, then scratched once behind his ear.

From inside the blacksmith's came the sound of huffing and sniffing, then a wet nose appeared at the crack at the bottom of the door. A moment later, the door swung open and the greyhound disappeared inside.

"Did anyone see you?" a beagle by the name of Stoker asked as he closed the door and looked up at the greyhound with worried eyes.

Stoker was always worried about something.

"No." The greyhound removed his cape. "I was not

followed."

Dresden relished his role as a messenger, doing his part to fight persecution. He had once been a slave in another land, forced to chase a mechanical rabbit around a track with other greyhounds for entertainment, but he had been set free by a group of vigilantes and escaped to Felinia. That had been before King Griffen had risen to power. Before the dark times.

Stoker led Dresden through a door into another room, where five other dogs sat waiting in the glow of a warm fire.

"What news?" Gwen asked. A beautiful and well-groomed golden retriever, Gwen sat near the fireplace, her eyes aglow.

"More bad than good," Dresden said before he leaned down to take a drink of water from the community bowl.

"Speak," Fedora said. A black and white border collie, Fedora was the unofficial leader of the revolution. "Speak so that we may judge what is good and what is not."

Dresden looked up, his muzzle wet and water dripping from his chin as he glanced around the fire lit room. In addition to Stoker the beagle, Gwen the golden retriever, and Fedora the border collie, three other dogs sat waiting to hear something that would give them hope: Bogart the Saint Bernard, Ian the Scottish terrier, and a German shepherd-wolf mix named Yancy.

They were all that remained of the revolution.

Dresden licked his chops and warmed himself by the fire. "The king has..."

"The king indeed," Bogart snorted.

Dresden ignored the Saint Bernard. "The king has secured our comrades on the second level of the dungeon while the Maiden Poodle occupies a cell on the lowermost level. A twenty-four-hour armed guard has been posted at the dungeon's door and at every entrance to the castle, with sentries posted every fifty meters along the castle wall."

"We are done then," Stoker whined. The beagle let out a howl of despair, then turned in three tight circles and slumped to the floor, his head on his paws. "It is hopeless."

"It is not hopeless," Gwen said. The golden retriever nudged Stoker with her nose to try to comfort him. "As long as there is one of us left, we are not done."

"But how can we be expected to defeat the king's army?" Stoker asked. "There are only seven of us."

"It is not a question of defeating them," Bogart said. The Saint Bernard looked around the room with an air of confidence. "If you ask me, they are already defeated."

"Fabulous!" Ian said. The Scottish terrier wagged his tail. "Our work is done. Where shall we have the victory party?"

Fedora shook her head. "This is no time for humor, Ian."

"Do tell me when it's time." Ian's tail drooped between

his hind legs. "I could so use a good laugh."

"Vut do you mean, 'zey are already defeated'?" Yancy asked, panting. The German shepherd-wolf mix was always panting.

"He means," Fedora said, "that their sheer volume of guards and the lengths the king has taken to secure the castle indicates that he recognizes us as a threat. We're inside his head. And that is half the battle." The border collie turned to Bogart. "Is that right?"

The Saint Bernard barked once and nodded, his tail thumping several times against the floor.

"Unfortunately," Ian said, "the other half of the battle needs to take place outside of this room. Nothing personal, but I wouldn't exactly give the seven of us good odds at storming the castle."

"I think you underestimate us." Fedora turned to the greyhound. "Dresden, deliver the rest of your news."

The news was not good. In addition to assembling his forces to protect the castle from an invasion, King Griffen had also determined that those rebels who had been captured would be charged with high treason. In two days' time they would all be put on trial, with those found guilty of crimes against the king to be executed post haste.

The seven dogs sat in the dark room, the fire fading along with their hopes. Stoker, who lay on the floor, put his paws over his nose and let out a small whine.

"You said your news was more bad than good," Gwen said. "Pray tell us what is good."

"It is no secret that the king and his sister do not get along," Dresden said.

"Aye," Ian said. "I hear they fight like cats and dogs."

Dresden nodded once. "Indeed. Not an hour ago word came that the princess is sympathetic to our plight."

A rumble of yips and barks arose from the rebels while Ian ran excitedly back and forth.

Fedora raised a paw to quiet them. The border collie turned to Dresden. "Is she willing to help us?"

"It is not a matter of will," the greyhound said. "It is a matter of opportunity."

"Then we must not delay," Fedora said. "We must do what we can to help the princess free our comrades."

"Agreed," Gwen said, her expression hopeful. But then, the golden retriever always seemed to have a smile on her face.

"But what can we do?" Stoker said, his eyes filled with worry.

"We will send word to the princess," Fedora said. "We will acknowledge her assistance, pledge our loyalty, and wait for her reply."

"What if it's a trap?" Bogart asked.

"It is a chance we must be willing to take," Fedora said. "These trials must not come to pass.

Chapter 3

As the rebels prepared their plans to send a message to the princess, King Griffen lay asleep in his bed—an enormous, four-poster canopy with an overstuffed down mattress and privacy veils. The king spent many hours in his luxurious bed, which makes one wonder how he or any cat could actually rule a kingdom since they slept all day long. But that is of no matter, for King Griffen did rule, and such was his fierce demeanor that none would dare to question him, not even his sister, the Princess Eponine.

A svelte, long-haired tortoiseshell with vibrant green eyes, the princess was often regarded as nothing more than just another pretty face. But Eponine was a shrewd and crafty feline who had learned to use her beauty to her advantage, allowing her to keep her intellect and intentions a secret. For the princess knew that any perceived challenge to her brother would land her in the dungeon or get her banished to The Valley of Despair.

Still, the princess knew that she could not continue to stand by and allow her brother to rule the kingdom with fear and an iron paw. She had to do something to stop him.

In addition to the rebel canines to whom she had sent word, Princess Eponine had enlisted the help of a few of her closest and most trusted feline consorts. But in order to dethrone her brother, the princess needed more than the remnants of the revolution or a few courageous cats. What she needed was a little magic.

While her brother slept in the lap of decadence and the sun crept above the mountains to the east, Princess Eponine walked along the castle's corridors, her head held high and her tail swishing playfully back and forth. She often made use of her beauty to charm the king's guards, most of whom were simple-minded cats who could be easily manipulated with a well-timed purr or a blink of her captivating green eyes. Some guards, however, presented more of a challenge.

The dungeon was currently guarded by one such guard: an orange flame point named Finn. Now Finn was married to Fanny, a flamboyant feline most ferocious. Fanny was famous throughout Felinia for her feral fetishes and fatal fangs. Due to Fanny's affinity to throw furious fits, Finn remained faithful, foregoing fickle flights of fancy that might lead to ill-fated fortune.

Thus was Princess Eponine's challenge when she arrived at the dungeon.

"Good morning, Finn." The princess greeted him with a swish of her tail.

Finn stood at attention, tail to the dungeon entrance, his pupils fully open. He gave a slight bow of his head but did not purr. "Good morning, your highness."

Princess Eponine knew that her charms alone would have no effect on Finn due to the fear instilled in him by his wife, so she chose to take a somewhat different approach.

"Are the prisoners awake?" the princess asked.

"Yes, your highness," Finn said. "They have been served their morning rations of stale kibble and dirty water."

"Good." The princess moved toward the door. "That will make my job easier."

Finn moved to block her. "I am sorry, your highness. But I am under strict orders from King Griffen to allow no one to pass without his permission."

"But I have my brother's permission," Princess Eponine said.

"I was not informed of it, your highness."

"I suppose you are only doing your job, Finn." The princess turned to leave. "I shall go wake my brother and bring him here so that you may verify his instructions."

Eponine knew that the thought of having a face-to-face

with King Griffen would likely terrify the flame point, and she couldn't help but smile as Finn began to stammer behind her.

"Your-your-your highness?"

She turned around. "Yes, Finn?"

"That will not be necessary, your highness."

"What will not be necessary?"

Finn removed the keys to the dungeon and unlocked the door. "Your word is good enough for me."

"Thank you, Finn." Princess Eponine gave the flame point a smile as she walked past him into the dungeon.

The dungeon consisted of three levels of prison cells, with the bars of each cell set less than two inches apart in order to prevent even the smallest Chihuahua or Pomeranian from escaping. On the first level of the dungeon were common criminals: thieves, vagrants, prowlers, howlers, biters, fighters, diggers, chewers, and a sheltie named Lulu who constantly barked at the garbage collector. At present the sixteen cells on the first level were filled to capacity, while the twenty cells on the second level held more than two-dozen rebel canines captured by the king's guards. The lowest level of the dungeon was smaller than the other two and had just six prison cells. Currently, only one of these cells was occupied.

As Princess Eponine approached the cell, even as she arrived on the lowest level, she began to feel a calm come over her—a warm, bewitching wave of air that seemed to flow around her and fill her with confidence, as if she had nothing to fear. In the dim light given off by the torches that lined the cold, damp, dungeon walls, she saw nothing but darkness and shadows. Then a voice called her name as if she were an old friend and her eyes followed the voice to the shape which lay upright, serene and untroubled, on the cell floor.

"Good morning, Princess," the Maiden Poodle said.

Princess Eponine stared in wonder at the regal black standard poodle, her posture and countenance a defiant yet sublime contrast to her austere and wretched surroundings. The princess found herself offering a small curtsey.

"Good morning," Princess Eponine said, her voice coming out barely more than a whisper. She had never been in the presence of such a magnificent creature. Courage and confidence radiated from the Maiden Poodle, filling the princess with both reverence and humility, for she had never encountered, nor imagined, such strength or power.

"You have come to offer assistance?" Camille asked.

"I have come to offer hope."

The Maiden Poodle smiled. "That is usually what others seek of me."

"Why do people seek you?" the princess asked.

"Because they believe I have the power to help them, to heal them, to answer their questions."

While the princess did not know anyone who had personally met the Maiden Poodle, she had heard the stories and rumors of her abilities. She had also heard that Camille was a descendant of sorcerers.

"Are you a sorceress?" the princess asked.

"No," Camille said. "Sorcery involves magic and magic is not at work within me."

"Then what are you?"

"I am a conduit," the poodle said. "A link between the world that you see and the world that you do not."

"Spirits?"

"Yes," Camille said. "But there is much that you do not see and spirits are but a small part of that world. For everything natural has a life force—the earth, the sky, the wind, the rain—and everything speaks through me."

Princess Eponine was in awe of this revelation and could not find the thoughts or words to express her astonishment. So instead she nervously licked her right paw and cleaned herself behind the ears.

"You said you came to offer hope," the Maiden Poodle said.

"Yes." The princess explained her plan to free Camille from the dungeon with the help of the remaining rebels, to whom she had sent word of her intentions.

"I have enlisted the aid of several allies who do not agree with my brother's actions and who, as I, wish to see him deposed," the princess said. "But I fear we cannot succeed in dethroning my brother without your unique abilities. Will you help us?"

"There is not much I can do from here," Camille said. "A dark and malevolent force lives within these stones and clouds the energy that flows through me."

During the reign of Queen Lilith, the dungeons were seldom used and the castle remained bright and warm beneath the queen's just and kind paw. Such an environment would not have hindered the Maiden Poodle's powers, even had the unlikely event of her imprisonment occurred, for it was well known that castles took on the personality of their rulers. But with the cold and pitiless rule of King Griffen emanating from the castle walls, the Maiden Poodle's powers remained subdued.

"Once outside of these walls, I will do what I can to help you and your friends," Camille said.

"Then I must act quickly," Princess Eponine said. "I shall contact the rebels and tell them to prepare to rendezvous with me as soon as possible."

The Maiden Poodle glanced over Princess Eponine's shoulder and shook her head. "I am afraid it is too late."

An instant later, several guards appeared at the base of the stairs, stepping to either side and standing at attention as King Griffen strolled past them into the dungeon.

"I see you have once again managed to manipulate one

of my guards," the king said.

King Griffen stood tall and muscular, with a large, solid body and a head one size too small. His coat was shiny and as black as the shadows in the dungeon, while his bright yellow eyes glowed with self-importance.

"My actions are driven by my conscience," the princess said. "Perhaps if you were driven by such noble ideals, I would not have to deceive your men."

"Well, this time you will pay for your insubordination," King Griffen said. "Guards!"

Two of the armed guards rushed over and seized the princess while the other two opened the door to the cell directly across from the Maiden Poodle. Moments later, Princess Eponine joined Camille as the only occupants of the dungeon's lowest level.

King Griffen approached the cell, bounding at it sideways with his back arched and his tail puffed up.

"You don't impress anyone with your silly displays," Princess Eponine said.

"I would watch the way you speak to your king if I were you."

"You are not my king," the princess said. "You are but a false ruler who does not deserve to sit on the throne."

King Griffen leaned close to the bars and hissed. "Perhaps when you are brought up on trial for treason you will consider begging for my mercy."

"You are incapable of mercy," the princess said.

"I find that to be one of my most endearing traits," King Griffen said with a smile before he turned and walked away from the cell and out of the dungeon.

Once the king and his guards had left, Princess Eponine sat at the front of her cell and looked across the corridor in despair, where the Maiden Poodle stood on her hind legs with her paws on the bars of her own cell.

"I am sorry, your highness," Camille said. "You should not have risked your freedom for mine."

"It is I who am sorry," Princess Eponine said. "I made the mistake of underestimating my brother. I'm afraid there is no way to stop him now."

"There is always a way," Camille said. "It is just a matter of finding it."

While the princess wanted to believe the Maiden Poodle, she didn't know how anyone would be able to find a way to rescue the rebels and dethrone her brother now. Any optimism she'd had was gone, as if the darkness had reached out and dragged her hopes into the shadows.

But beyond the castle and the borders of the kingdom, in the remote reaches of Felinia, hope still existed.

Chapter 4

Beyond the low-lying yet formidable mountains that rimmed the kingdom of Felinia was The Valley of Despair, where the outcasts of Felinia lived. Fabled to be a harsh and desolate place where hardship dwelled and misery reigned, The Valley of Despair was never spoken of loudly or in public but in whispers laced with reverence and fear, as those who were sent beyond the familiar mountains of the kingdom were never heard from nor seen again.

Because of its reputation, and because of the alleged treacherous journey to reach it, The Valley of Despair remained untouched and unseen by those who did not live within its natural walls. As such, its true nature remained steeped in folklore, with the myths created not by the king nor by any of the kingdom's residents, but by the inhabitants of The Valley of Despair itself.

Overgrown with lush vegetation and fed by three separate waterfalls that converged into a single lake, the valley, in truth, knew little of despair. Food and water were plentiful, the weather was never too hot nor too cold, and cats and dogs co-existed in a society in which no one was wealthy and no one went without. Not even a cat who had once been a prince could expect to find royal treatment here.

The red Persian, fresh from his monthly grooming at The Valley of Despair Cat Grooming Shoppe, strolled along the promenade overlooking the blue, serene lake. Prince Atticus could remember a time not long before when his afternoon walks would take him through the hallways of the castle or along the wall overlooking the moat. Occasionally he would venture into the village, but his entourage always accompanied him and he would often spend half of his time signing autographs and taking pictures with tourists.

The uncle of Princess Eponine and King Griffen, Prince Atticus was the brother of Queen Lilith the Just and had been named by the queen as the heir to assume the throne upon her passing. A fair, benevolent, and well-loved prince, his coronation was to be a celebration to help heal the kingdom after the passing of the queen.

However, days before the coronation was to take place, a story appeared in the *Daily Mews*, Felinia's local tabloid newspaper, claiming that Prince Atticus was not of noble blood.

According to the story, the prince was the offspring of a commoner and had been left in a basket one night outside the main gate, where he was found and adopted by the royal family and raised as one of their own. The prince had no more royal blood in him than a common tomcat.

The scandal rocked Felinia. After a short trial, overseen and ruled upon by his nephew, Prince Atticus was found guilty of impersonating a royal cat and banished from the kingdom forever. The following day, Griffen was crowned the new King of Felinia.

Prince Atticus had no doubts that his nephew, who had expected to be named king, had planted the story about him in order to sabotage his coronation. But the prince had been unable to get any evidence to prove any wrongdoing by his nephew, so he had left Felinia and made his way to The Valley of Despair.

At times Atticus missed the familiarity and celebrity of his former life, the comforts that went with it, and those he loved—particularly his niece, Princess Eponine. But all in all, being banished by his petulant nephew had been the best thing that could have happened to him, for Atticus enjoyed the freedom and simplicity of his new life and the anonymity that came with it.

Although none of the adults ever made reference to his royal lineage, they nonetheless paid Atticus a great deal of respect. Many of the youngsters, however, delighted in calling him 'the Atticus formerly known as Prince'.

He continued his afternoon stroll along the promenade, past a group of puppies and kittens playing tag around a small grove of palm trees, chasing their tails and each other. One of the youngsters, a white poodle puppy whom Atticus had never seen before, broke away from the others and came over to him.

"Your highness," the poodle said, bowing gracefully before him on its forelegs.

"I am not anyone's highness, child," Atticus said.

The poodle straightened up. "And I am not a child."

The poodle's voice suddenly struck Atticus as too deep for that of a puppy. It was only when the Persian looked into the eyes of the poodle that he realized his mistake. This was no puppy. This was a full-grown poodle in miniature.

In Felinia, poodles were rare creatures. Less than five had ever called Felinia home, and as far back as Atticus could remember, he had never seen nor heard of a miniature poodle. This was a first indeed.

"Who are you?" the prince asked.

"I come to you on the gravest of errands, your highness," the poodle said. "May we speak in private?"

Atticus led the miniature white poodle to a secluded area of the promenade, away from the children and passers-by.

"I repeat," Atticus said. "Who *are* you?"

"Forgive me for being short on etiquette, your highness," the poodle said, bowing once again. "You may call me Vincent."

"And you may quit calling me 'your highness'," Atticus said.

"If it pleases you."

"It does please me," Atticus said. "Now what is this grave matter of which you speak?"

"I hail from the land of Watonia," Vincent said. "Perhaps you have heard of it."

"Yes," Atticus said. "I have heard of it."

Watonia was rumored to be an enchanted land, its inhabitants imbued with special powers that included magic and mind-reading. Though not all poodles hailed from Watonia, those who did possessed powers far greater than all of the other creatures who called Watonia home.

"You are correct," Vincent said.

"Correct about what?" Atticus asked.

"Your thoughts," Vincent said. "It is true that I and my brothers and sisters possess powers far beyond others from our land."

The red Persian could do nothing but remain speechless, for he had never before had anyone read his thoughts.

"I apologize if I have made you uneasy," Vincent said.

"We are not in the habit of showing off. However, I felt I must make my powers clear for you to understand the importance of why I have come."

"Please," Atticus said. "Explain yourself so that I may understand."

"As I said, I hail from Watonia," the miniature poodle said. "And, as you rightfully assume, I, like my brothers and sisters, have special powers beyond the scope of most mortals, powers that we use for the benefit of our land and those who inhabit it. Likewise, when the situation arises, we help those in other lands to achieve peace and harmony; which leads me to the matter for which I seek your assistance."

"My assistance?" Prince Atticus said.

"Several years ago a poodle was born, a black standard poodle named Camille. Upon her birth, it was obvious that she possessed powers far beyond those previously seen in our or any other breed. Great things were expected of her and she did not disappoint, complementing her powers with an uncanny intelligence and a deep sense of compassion."

"The Maiden Poodle," Atticus said.

"You have met her?"

The red Persian gave a shake of his head. "I have only heard of her, and only then before I was...before I came to live here."

"So then you know not of her fate?" Vincent said.

"Of what fate do you speak?"

"She has been taken prisoner by the king, your nephew, and in two days' time will be put on trial for treason," Vincent said. "It is unlikely she will be found innocent."

Any trace of the good mood Atticus had enjoyed was swept away by the miniature poodle's pronouncement, for he knew what fate awaited those found guilty of treason. Banishment to The Valley of Despair would not be an option.

Atticus regarded Vincent with a somber scowl. But then he was a Persian. He always looked like he was scowling. "What is it you have come to ask of me?"

"I have come to request your help in rescuing the Maiden Poodle."

"Rescue?" Prince Atticus said, then laughed. "I believe you have the wrong cat."

"A small group of those willing and able to defy the king are prepared to risk what they have, but they cannot succeed alone," Vincent said. "You are the only one who knows the inside of the castle. Without your assistance, the others will be walking into a trap."

"Can you not use your powers to free the Maiden Poodle?" the prince asked.

"Unfortunately, my powers do not extend to physical feats," Vincent said. "They are limited to mind-reading and a few other tricks that, while useful and fun at parties, are not by themselves practical in this situation. In addition, any psychic advantage I might have is limited by the castle, which is imbued with a dark, negative energy that I am unable to overcome."

The prince nodded. "That would be the work of my nephew."

"So will you help me?"

The prince thought about how out of shape he was, how tired he often grew, how old he had become. He had no desire to return to the kingdom, to confront his nephew and put on the hero's hat. He simply wanted to remain in The Valley of Despair and live out a simple, comfortable life. Could the miniature poodle not find someone else?

"No," Vincent said. "There is no one else."

Atticus would have blushed with embarrassment at having his cowardly thoughts read by Vincent, but cats don't blush. Especially red Persians.

"What about my niece?" Prince Atticus said. "She knows the castle as well as I do. Surely she would be willing to help."

"Princess Eponine attempted to help the Maiden Poodle but was discovered by her brother," Vincent said. "She has been taken prisoner and awaits trial for treason, as well."

A pair of Siamese kittens bounded past, stopping long enough to call out to Prince Atticus, saying something that made both of the kittens laugh playfully before they bounded off, but the prince didn't hear them. All he could see, all he could imagine, was his niece caged in a dark cell.

"Time is running short, your highness," Vincent said.

Prince Atticus had always been of an easy-going nature, never creating conflict nor searching out a confrontation, and more often than not keeping his opinions to himself. When his nephew had concocted the story of illegitimacy that had taken away the throne and led to his exile, Atticus had put up little resistance and simply accepted his fate.

He would not accept this.

"When do we leave?" the prince asked.

"At once," Vincent said.

And so Prince Atticus left The Valley of Despair with Vincent, the miniature white poodle, to make the journey back to the kingdom and free the princess and the Maiden Poodle.

He hoped he would not arrive too late.

Chapter 5

As night fell across the kingdom, the rebels gathered together at the home of Gwen the golden retriever to discuss what they were to do now that Princess Eponine had been imprisoned.

"Without zee princess, how are vee supposed to rescue zee others?" Yancy asked, panting as usual. "Vee have no vun who can get us inside."

"And with the trials little more than a day away, we are running out of time," Bogart said. The Saint Bernard emphasized his frustration with a single thump of his large paw.

"It seems hopeless," Stoker said. The beagle laid his chin on the table and sighed.

"We must not give up hope," Fedora said. The border collie looked around the room at the others. "Hope is all we have right now. We must all believe in it and embrace it or we are done for."

Silence settled on the room, with the only sounds that of Yancy panting and the flames crackling in the fireplace. A knock at the back door brought them all to attention and caused Stoker to bark and whine.

"Stoker," Fedora said. "Remain calm."

"Sorry," Stoker said, his ears and tail drooping. "I have a high excitability rating."

Gwen padded to the back door. Moments later the golden retriever returned with Dresden, who was panting like a dog.

"Look what the cat dragged in," Ian said.

"A cat?" Stoker ran and hid behind Bogart. "I'm afraid of cats."

"It's just an expression," the Saint Bernard said, shooting Ian a scowl. "And a poorly chosen one, at that."

"Just trying to lighten the mood a wee bit," the Scottish terrier said.

"There is a time for play and a time to be serious," Fedora said. "We would all do well to know the difference."

Ian huffed and started chewing on a bone as Fedora turned to Dresden. "What news this time?"

The greyhound finished drinking from a bowl of water, then proceeded to tell the others about the miniature poodle from the land of Watonia who had traveled to The Valley of

Despair to fetch Prince Atticus.

"Fetch," Ian said. "That's a good one."

None of the other dogs found him amusing.

"How did this miniature poodle know of our plight?" Fedora asked.

"I do not know," Dresden said. "But it's my understanding that he learned of our troubles through sorcery."

This wasn't too far from the truth, for Vincent had received a telepathic message from the Maiden Poodle prior to her imprisonment and arrived in Felinia in time to ascertain the dilemma facing the rebels. He knew before they did that Prince Atticus was their only hope.

"All I know is that he is supposed to bring the prince here tomorrow and we are to meet them at the toymaker's cottage at the corner of Hiss and Purr," Dresden said. "There we are to plan our rescue."

"When are they to arrive?" Gwen asked.

Dresden scratched at himself, which he had been doing a lot lately, making all of the others nervous. None of them liked the idea of catching fleas. "With any luck they will arrive tomorrow at sunset."

A clamor of excited barks and howls arose among the rebels, with Ian and Stoker turning around in small circles.

Fedora raised a paw to quiet them. "It is settled, then. We will meet at the toymaker's cottage tomorrow at dusk."

"Zis toymaker?" Yancy asked. "Iz he to be trusted?"

"The word of a poodle from Watonia is good enough for me," Bogart said.

"And me," Gwen said.

"Aye, lassie," Ian said. "Count me in, as well."

The rest of the rebels agreed. And while there was still a great amount of trepidation regarding the events that were yet to transpire and the fate of their friends, they also felt a sense of excitement. This proved to be a problem for Stoker, who suffered from Excitement Urination Syndrome and often piddled when he received good news.

"You need to get that under control, laddie," Ian said.

In spite of Stoker's awkward doggie faux pas, the rebels spent the evening in good spirits, hopeful and anticipating the arrival of Prince Atticus and Vincent, the sorcerer poodle. Yancy, the German shepherd-wolf mix, panted and licked his chops repeatedly in apparent excitement over the news before he bid everyone *gute nacht,* slipped away into the night and, once he was certain no one was watching, headed toward the castle.

Chapter 6

King Griffen lay stretched out on his back across his royal bed, paws curled up to his chest, his whiskers and paws twitching as he dreamt of bounding through an open field, chasing mice. In his dream he caught one of the creatures by the tail, batted at it, then let it go and pounced after it, continuing his game of cat and mouse. Just as he prepared to pounce again, the ground began to shake and a roar filled the air. King Griffen looked up and saw a giant mouse, as big as a dragon, thundering toward him across the field.

He awoke to the sound of a knocking at his door.

"Who disturbs me?" King Griffen growled. He rolled over onto his paws and stretched, shaking the dream from his undersized head before leaping to the floor.

"It is I, your highness," came the voice of the guard

from beyond the door.

"I know it is you," the king said, marching to the door and opening it to reveal a gray and white tabby standing at attention. "Who else would knock at my door but the soldier responsible for guarding it?"

"I do not know, your highness." The guard, a young cat by the name of Waldo, glanced around with a look of confusion. "I am the only one here."

"That is apparent," King Griffen said. "And as you are the only one here, no one else should knock on this door unless you allow them to pass."

"Oh, that would never happen, your highness," Waldo said. "I am the only one who would knock on your door."

King Griffen clicked his claws impatiently against the stone floor. "What do you want, you incompetent fool? Why do you disturb me?"

"Were you expecting someone, your highness?" Waldo asked.

"I am expecting no one."

"Ah. Then I shall instruct your visitor to leave."

"What visitor?" King Griffen asked.

"It is of no matter," Waldo said. "As you were not expecting anyone, I shall escort him out."

"Tell me who the visitor is!" King Griffen growled. "Unless you would prefer to join my sister in the dungeon."

"No, your highness. I would not prefer that." Waldo

looked around again before he leaned forward in a conspiratorial whisper. "There's a dog to see you, your highness."

"A dog?" The king's back arched and his tail puffed up. "What breed of dog?"

"A foreigner, your highness," Waldo said. "He has a German accent."

King Griffen relaxed. "Very well. Show this mongrel in before I change my mind and send you to the dungeon anyway."

"Right away, your highness."

King Griffen closed the door to his chamber and paced about the room, stopping to scratch his claws on his bedpost before suddenly running off in pursuit of some invisible creature, as cats are often inclined to do. Even kings of Felinia.

A knock at the door brought his antics to an end.

"Enter," King Griffen said, sitting dignified with his characteristic arrogance.

The door opened and Waldo escorted in Yancy, the German shepherd-wolf mix who, as usual, was panting.

"Leave us," the king said.

Waldo bowed once and closed the door, leaving the king and Yancy alone.

"Why have you come here?" the king hissed, walking past the mixed breed with an imperious swish of his tail.

"You were instructed to contact me through anonymous channels."

"Ya, I apologize, your highness," Yancy said. "But dis matter for vich I come could not vait."

"I shall be the judge of what can or cannot wait." King Griffen walked around in a circle until he stood facing Yancy, staring at him, pupils full and black.

Several weeks prior to his ascension to the throne, Griffen, who at the time had still been a prince, met Yancy in the dungeon, where the penitent dog had been jailed for the night after drinking out of a public toilet and digging in his neighbor's yard.

"I have a proposition for you," Prince Griffen had said before producing a Beggin' Strip and waving it in front of the bars to Yancy's cell.

The German shepherd-wolf mix had watched the Beggin' Strip attentively, his head moving back and forth and his tongue hanging out, his eyes never leaving the fake bacon treat. "Ya, I'm listening."

Prince Griffen had smiled, then offered a year's supply of Beggin' Strips to Yancy for his help in planting evidence that would get his uncle banished from the kingdom.

"Vy vould you vant to banish your own uncle?" Yancy had asked.

"Are you questioning me?" Prince Griffen had said.

Yancy had shaken his head, whether in answer to the

question or because he couldn't take his eyes off the Beggin'
Strip, it was never known.

"Good boy," Prince Griffen had said, then tossed a piece
of Beggin' Strip to Yancy, who had gobbled it down without
chewing. "Now here's what you're going to do…"

From that moment forward, Yancy had become
Griffen's personal spy, informing him of the revolution and
of the rebels' plans, even providing many of the names of
the dogs King Griffen's guards had captured. But while the
king liked to be kept up to date, he did not like having his
cat naps interrupted.

"Now tell me what has compelled you to appear before
me and disturb my sleep." King Griffen stood in the middle
of his chamber and stared at the German shepherd-wolf
mix. "If I am not satisfied with your answer, then you shall
find yourself with the other traitors in the dungeon."

Yancy related the news regarding Prince Atticus and the
miniature poodle Vincent, who were expected to arrive
from The Valley of Despair the following day under cover of
night. At an emergency meeting, a plan would be devised
for the rescue of Princess Eponine and the Maiden Poodle,
along with the other prisoners. Once the canines had
liberated their comrades and taken them to a safe house,
they would attempt to remove the king from Felinia's
throne.

King Griffen scratched at his chin, his eyes narrowing

and his tail twitching. "Where is this meeting to occur?"

"At zee toymaker's cottage," Yancy said. "At zee corner of Hiss and Purr."

"The toymaker's cottage," King Griffen said. "How perfectly apropos. You mongrels are like children."

"Ya, my lord, if you say so."

"And since they are but children," the king said, "then we shall play a game. Not for fun or sport or prizes, but for my amusement, just the same."

The king leapt onto his bed and lay upon silk so fine. "You will arrive at this meeting with word that I have learned of its design. Apparently, you'll say, there is a traitor, a startling revelation. This will undoubtedly be followed by claw-pointing and rampant accusation."

Yancy nodded in excitement and opened his mouth to pant as he listened to King Griffen, who continued with his rant.

"And while the meeting is in chaos amid charges of subversion, my guards will arrive and arrest the lot, including my uncle, the flat-faced Persian."

"And vut of me?" the shepherd-wolf mix asked. "Am I to be seized as vell?"

"It's unavoidable," the king said. "But do not fear, for your freedom you will not sell. I will show mercy to those who profess their loyalty to the throne, and for your obedience I will throw you more than just a bone."

The king produced a bag of Beggin' Strips and tossed it to the floor, and like most dogs all Yancy could think of was that he wanted more.

"Thank you, your highness," Yancy said, as he bent one forepaw and bowed. The king looked down from upon his bed, dignified and proud.

"Now leave me," King Griffen said. "For you are in need of a bath. And do not fail me or you shall know the full extent of my wrath."

Once Yancy left, King Griffen called in Waldo and told his guard to gather a dozen soldiers for a mission. "Or two dozen, if you'd rather."

The mission would take place that night, the details he conveyed, then the king sent Waldo back to his post and called the chamber maid. Fresh linens she provided, fresh pillows for his head, and then the maid left the king alone atop his massive bed.

The king sat and pondered briefly on the events that were to come, then he yawned and stretched and cleaned himself from his ears down to his bum. He had no doubts about his fate, no worries and no fears. His rule would earn him wealth and power and last for years and years.

From a golden saucer the king lapped up a stomach-full of cream, then he sprawled out upon his massive bed and fell asleep to dream.

Chapter 7

In the dungeon beneath the castle, Princess Eponine stood at the front of her cell, attempting to squeeze her narrow body through the even narrower bars. But as svelte as she was, she could not fit. Frustrated, she returned to the middle of her cell and started grooming herself. She couldn't help it. When she got nervous, she groomed.

"You should save your energy, Princess," the Maiden Poodle said from her cell.

"I fail to see what I should save it for," Princess Eponine said before she spit out a mouthful of cat hair. "My brother will not spare my life, nor is it likely he will spare yours."

"Perhaps not," Camille said. "But he cannot take what you do not give him."

Princess Eponine stared through the gloom of the dungeon into the other cell and wondered, not for the first time, how the poodle could remain so calm.

"You do not know my brother," the princess said. "He has a history of taking whatever he wants."

"He cannot take your spirit," the Maiden Poodle said. "Nor can he take the force that creates what you know as life."

"But that's exactly what he intends to take," the princess said. "My life."

"Then he is mistaken."

Princess Eponine scratched once distractedly behind her left ear, then stared at the Maiden Poodle with a blank expression. "I do not understand."

"The energy which imbues your physical form is not restricted by any boundaries," Camille said. "It remains in everything you touch and all that you encounter. Even now it flows from you into the stones beneath your paws."

Princess Eponine looked down at the floor of her cell and lifted one of her paws, sniffed at it, then returned her blank expression to the Maiden Poodle.

Camille closed her eyes. For a moment Princess Eponine believed that the Maiden Poodle had grown tired of their discussion and had chosen to take a nap. But a moment later, something began to press against Princess Eponine's paw from one of the stones directly beneath her.

The princess leapt back with a startled hiss, tail puffed up and back arched as she watched a strange, worm-like creature emerge from the stone. As the creature grew from two inches to six inches to ten inches tall, it turned from black to brown to green and sprouted several appendages that themselves sprouted even smaller appendages, at the end of which appeared numerous, delicate oval-shapes. All the while the creature continued to grow, now more than twelve inches tall—a dark, vibrant green with a head the size of a walnut. A moment later, the head of the creature split on several sides and then burst open in a brilliant ivory display.

Princess Eponine watched the creature, preparing to pounce. But once the creature had stopped growing, the princess stared at it, unable to say anything for several moments. She realized it wasn't any kind of creature at all but...

"A rose," the princess whispered in awe, standing up and drawing closer, sniffing the pure white petals with a tentative twitch of her nose. "But how...?"

"Life is in everything," the Maiden Poodle said. "It flows continuously, from you to the stone and back again. It is a never-ending cycle that not even your brother can break."

"But the rose?" the princess asked. "How did you make it grow?"

"I did not make it grow," Camille said. "It grew on its own. I simply called to the rose and it answered."

"Then we are not without hope," the princess said. "If you can call a flower from a stone, escape is within our grasp!"

The Maiden Poodle shook her head. "Calling to a rose does not take much strength, and I'm afraid I cannot do much more than that. Without the sun to nourish me, my powers grow weak and the darkness grows stronger."

The princess shivered—not from the cold nor from the dampness of the dungeon, but from the images conjured by the Maiden Poodle's words.

"What do you mean?" Princess Eponine asked, not truly knowing if she wanted to hear the answer.

"Natural sunlight replenishes my energy, allowing me to perform such feats as what you just witnessed," Camille said. "The darkness, however, drains the energy from me, increasing its own power."

For the first time Princess Eponine noticed how tired Camille appeared and how much darker the dungeon had become.

"I thought you said the energy of life is a never-ending cycle," the princess said. "That no one can take it from you."

"That is so," the Maiden Poodle said. "But the darkness is not a living creature. It is an organism unlike any other. Within its boundaries the darkness holds many gateways to worlds unknown to us, worlds inhabited by beings that are not governed by the laws of our world."

Princess Eponine shivered again and glanced nervously at the shadows in the corners of her cell.

"My brothers and sisters and I are the guardians of the light," Camille continued. "Our very presence insures that there is balance in the world. The darkness is always attempting to spread across the oceans and continents and we work to keep it in check. For centuries we have succeeded, but lately I have sensed the darkness growing stronger. And if I and my lineage were to perish or be banished forever to a place without light, then darkness would prevail upon our world."

The princess could think of nothing to say, for she had never imagined the possibility of such things. She could almost feel the darkness sliding past her, caressing her paws and ears and fur with its cold touch, feeding upon her. She looked at Camille and noticed the shadows beginning to swirl around the poodle like a low, dense fog.

"Is there nothing you can do to stop this?" the princess asked, rubbing against the ivory rose for comfort. "Is there no way to get a message to anyone who can help?"

"I have done all that I can," the Maiden Poodle said as she laid her chin upon her forelegs and closed her eyes, the shadows swirling about her. "We can only wait and see what happens."

Chapter 8

Once the sun had set and the shadows had stretched out full and black across Felinia, the rebel canines gathered at the toymaker's cottage to discuss the rescue of the Maiden Poodle and to await the arrival of Prince Atticus and Vincent. Ian stood at the window, peeking out between the shutters, his tail wagging in anticipation, while Stoker paced back and forth behind him.

"Do you see them yet?" the beagle asked.

Ian turned and gave Stoker an exasperated glance. "How many times are you going to ask me that?"

"I can't help it," Stoker said. "When I have to wait, I get anxious."

"Then perhaps it would be a good idea to put down a pee pad," Ian said.

"We're all a little on edge," Fedora said. The border

collie walked over to Ian and placed a paw on the Scottie's shoulder. "I think we would all do well to show some patience."

"Aye, lassie," Ian said. He turned to Stoker and bowed his head. "My apologies. I meant no disrespect."

"It's okay," Stoker said and wagged his tail. "Do you see them yet?"

"Dresden will bring them here safely," Bogart said. "We have no need to worry."

Gwen bounded around the room, unable to control her excitement. "We are on the brink of a new dawn," the golden retriever said. "And soon we will be joined by Prince Atticus and a wizard from Watonia!"

"Is he truly a wizard?" Stoker asked.

"I believe that is so," Fedora said. "But I remind all of you to behave yourselves when they arrive. We do not have any time for nonsense."

Less than twelve hours remained before the trials were to commence and the severity of the situation was not lost on any of those present.

"Do you see them yet?" Stoker asked.

Ian turned to glare at the beagle as the toymaker entered the room carrying a tray of treats.

A black Labrador by the name of Popo Santiago, the toymaker had once lived on a remote tropical island where he made toys from coconut trees. After several years of selling his toys to the island's natives and getting hit on the head with one too many coconuts, Popo bought passage on a sailing vessel that brought him to Felinia. Born from a long line of crafters, Popo was well known throughout the village for his toys, particularly for their durability to withstand being chewed upon. He also baked delicious homemade dog biscuits.

"Would anyone like some more water or biscuits?" Popo asked.

A knocking at the back door precluded any response, except for Stoker, who let out a short series of barks before Fedora silenced him. All eyes turned to Ian.

"I didn't see anyone," the Scottie said. "They must have come by a different route."

Bogart snorted. "Maybe if you would cut your hair once in a while, you would be able to see past your bangs." The Saint Bernard walked through the doorway and disappeared into the back of the cottage. Moments later he returned with Yancy, who was panting heavily.

"Vee must leave at vonce," the shepherd-wolf mix said.

The rebels' barks and yips rose together in confusion and alarm.

"Leave?" Fedora said, her voice quieting the others. "Why? What has happened?"

"Vee have been betrayed," Yancy said.

"Betrayed?" Ian said.

Yancy nodded. "Zee king has learned of our meeting and is sending armed guards at zis very moment."

"Guards?" Stoker said.

At that moment, the pee pad Ian had recommended for Stoker would have come in handy.

"Who has betrayed us?" Bogart asked.

Before Yancy could answer, a pounding came at the front door.

Stoker let out a high-pitched whine and ran, terrified, through the other doorway toward the back of the cottage, piddling as he went. The others all sat and looked to each other, stunned and hopeless. Yancy's panting grew heavier.

With reluctance, Popo Santiago approached the front door and opened it, stepping aside as Waldo, King Griffen's personal guard, entered and closed the door behind him. Stoker returned to the room an instant later, stumbling through the other doorway as two armed feline guards appeared behind him.

"What is the meaning of this?" Fedora asked, though even without the news from Yancy, she knew full well that there could be only one purpose for a visit from King Griffen's guards.

"We have come to arrest those who would betray the throne of Felinia," Waldo said. The tabby looked at the other guards—a lanky Russian blue shorthair and a stout white and grey longhair—and nodded.

The two guards approached Yancy and seized the German shepherd-wolf mix.

Yancy let out a yelp. "Vut is the meaning of zis?"

"Do you have a cellar, toymaker?" Waldo asked.

Popo Santiago nodded obediently. "Yes, sir."

"And does it have a lock?" Waldo asked.

"It does," the black Labrador said.

"Then I would ask you to lead my comrades to your cellar so that they may lock up this traitor," Waldo said.

"Yes, sir," Popo said, his tail wagging. "This way."

Ian leaned over to Gwen. "Looks like someone's in the doghouse."

"Shush," the golden retriever said.

Once the other two guards had taken Yancy and followed the toymaker from the room, Waldo turned to face the others.

"I do not understand," Fedora said. "What is going on?"

Waldo smiled. "As I said, we have come to arrest those who would betray the throne of Felinia."

At that moment, Prince Atticus walked into the room from the back of the cottage, flanked by the greyhound, Dresden, and by Vincent, the miniature white poodle.

"Your highness," Waldo said, bowing before Prince Atticus.

The others in the room all followed suit.

"There is no time for formalities," Prince Atticus said.

"According to my friend here, we have much to do."

"I couldn't agree more, your highness," Fedora said. "But I believe I speak for everyone here when I say that we are somewhat confused."

"Perhaps I can explain," Waldo said as the other two guards returned from the basement with the toymaker. "Your friend, the one named Yancy, has conspired against you with King Griffen."

Several yips of surprise arose from the rebels.

"I had my doubts about him," Bogart said.

Ian nodded. "My father always said, never trust a half-breed."

"The king charged me with the responsibility of arresting all of you," Waldo said. "Fortunately, my brothers and I are loyal to Princess Eponine and to the throne, not to the imposter sitting upon it. We long for the days of Queen Lilith and wish to restore the throne to Prince Atticus."

With that, Waldo and the two guards bowed once again.

"I appreciate your loyalty," Prince Atticus said. "I would consider it an honor to know your names."

"My name is Waldo," he said. "And these are my brothers, Dino and Neo."

The Russian blue and the gray and white bowed their heads to the prince.

"And although I have met my escort," Prince Atticus said, motioning to Dresden, "I would consider it an honor to know the names of those who have worked so hard and suffered so much in my absence."

Once the introductions were completed, Popo Santiago brought out another tray of water and biscuits for everyone to share, as he had been taught to be a consummate host regardless of the circumstances. Every now and then, however, he would chase his tail in the middle of the room, creating an awkward moment when the others could only stare and shake their heads.

"We are grateful for your help," Fedora said to Prince Atticus and to Vincent. "And for yours, as well." She nodded to the three royal guards. "But we are in desperate need of a plan as we are uncertain how we can rescue the princess and the Maiden Poodle."

"I may have an idea," Prince Atticus said.

All eyes turned to the prince, except for Popo, who was cleaning himself in a manner that would more appropriately be conducted in private.

"There is a secret passage," the prince said. "It leads from a hidden door near the west gate and runs beneath the moat into the castle in the lowermost level of the dungeon. The passage was built as an escape route for the royal family were the castle ever to be seized."

"Who else knows of this passage?" Vincent asked.

"No one other than my niece, my nephew, and myself," Prince Atticus said.

"It is the first I have heard of it," Waldo said. Dino and Neo nodded their agreement before they started grooming themselves.

"So we can enter the dungeon, free our comrades, and bring them back through the secret passage without anyone knowing we were there," Bogart said.

"Unfortunately, it's not as simple as that," Prince Atticus said. "The passage was designed with cats in mind, so it is too small to accommodate large breeds of canines."

"Then what are we to do?" Stoker whined.

Vincent turned to Waldo. "Can you get the main dungeon door open?"

"The king has tightened security since the princess tricked her way past one of the guards," Waldo said. "While we have several additional sympathizers within the castle who can help us, it would be difficult to gain access to the dungeon without drawing attention."

Vincent looked from Waldo and his two feline brothers to the rebel canines. "Perhaps attention is what we want," the miniature poodle said.

"What are you thinking?" Fedora asked.

"I presume the king is expecting his guards to return with prisoners," Vincent said.

Waldo nodded. "Yes. If we do not return soon, he may grow suspicious and send out additional guards."

"If you showed up with fewer prisoners than he was

expecting, could you devise an excuse that would satisfy him as to what happened to the others?" Vincent asked.

Waldo's whiskers twitched. "Yes, I believe I could come up with something."

Vincent looked at the rebel canines. "Would any of you be willing to volunteer as prisoners?"

While Stoker let out a soft whimper and tucked his tail between his legs, Bogart, Gwen, Dresden, and Fedora each let out a single bark of affirmation. Ian stood on all fours and nodded, his tail standing at attention.

Vincent turned to Waldo and his two brothers. "Once you reach the dungeon, can you get the keys to the cells?"

Waldo and Neo both nodded. Dino coughed up a hairball, which wasn't exactly the answer anyone was looking for, but then he nodded, as well.

"Your highness, how large of a dog can fit through the secret passage?" Vincent asked.

Prince Atticus pondered this a moment. "It cannot accommodate a dog much larger than a miniature schnauzer or a Scottish terrier."

Everyone looked at Ian, who started wagging his tail involuntarily.

"So we could use the secret passage to help the smaller dogs escape," Bogart said.

"But that will still leave a number of our comrades trapped inside," Dresden said.

"Along with us," Gwen said.

Fedora nodded. "And the Maiden Poodle."

"Which means the rest of us would have to leave the castle through the main gate," Bogart said. "Past all of the king's guards."

Everyone fell silent as they pondered their dwindling options for success.

Fedora turned to Waldo. "How many of us would you need to pose as prisoners to convince the king?"

Waldo considered this a moment. "Three should be enough."

"Then Bogart, Gwen and I will go," Fedora said. The border collie looked to the Saint Bernard and the golden retriever. "If you are still willing."

Bogart and Gwen nodded their agreement.

"What about the rest of us?" Ian asked.

"Ian, you will accompany Prince Atticus and Vincent through the secret passage and help to lead the smaller dogs and Princess Eponine out of the dungeon," Fedora said. "Dresden, we will need your skills to lead the others to safety once they emerge from the passage."

The greyhound gave an obedient nod.

"What about me?" Stoker asked.

Fedora placed a paw on the beagle's shoulder. "You will stay with Dresden and help to see that our comrades are safe."

"The rest of us may have to fight our way out," Bogart said.

"Yes, it is risky," Fedora said. "Some of us may not return."

Stoker let out a mournful howl as the small band of rebels regarded each other with a combination of admiration and fear, for they had never before faced such a daunting task.

Vincent looked around the room at the six rebel canines and the four felines, then turned his attention to the toymaker, who sat on the floor cleaning himself near a selection of his hand-crafted cat toys.

The miniature poodle smiled. "Perhaps there is another way."

Chapter 9

In the pre-dawn hours of the morning that heralded the trials, six figures walked across the drawbridge and approached the front gate of the castle—three dogs and three cats who carried the weight of a kingdom upon their backs.

Waldo took the lead. Directly behind him in handcuffs walked Gwen, flanked by Fedora and Bogart.

"I hope this charade works," the Saint Bernard said.

"Do not hope," Fedora whispered. "To hope means there is a chance of failure. We cannot fail."

"Just be yourselves," Dino said, who brought up the rear with his brother, Neo. "Try not to act suspicious."

"I'm a one-hundred-and-ninety-pound Saint Bernard," Bogart said. "The very idea that I could be captured by a ten-pound cat is suspicious enough."

Dino puffed up. "I'll have you know I weigh eleven-and-one-quarter pounds."

Neo looked at his brother, impressed. "Have you been working out?"

"That and lots of kibble," Dino said. "It's loaded with carbs."

"Cut the chatter," Waldo said as they approached the main gate. "We're here."

Gwen glanced back and watched as the drawbridge drew up behind them. The golden retriever let out a soft whimper as it locked into place.

"Be strong," Fedora whispered.

The six of them walked through the main gate into a vaulted foyer guarded by half a dozen felines, one of whom stood at the base of a stone staircase that wound its way up into shadows. No sooner had the rebels entered the foyer when the portcullis lowered behind them, hitting the stone floor with an ominous *thud*. Moments later, King Griffen descended the stairs, ostentatious in a ruby-studded crown and a velvet robe that flowed out behind him.

"Your highness," Waldo said as he and his brothers bowed.

King Griffen approached, imperious and self-important as always. "Well well, what do we have here?"

"Prisoners, your highness," Waldo said. "Remember? You told me to bring them to you."

"I know what they are," King Griffen said. "I was just...never mind." He looked around, his expression turning from arrogant triumph to angry disappointment. "There are only three of them."

"Yes, sir," Waldo said. "That's the number I came up with, as well."

The king's claws clicked impatiently against the stone floor. "Where are the others?"

"The others?" Waldo asked.

"The other rebels!" The king turned on Waldo with a hiss, his pupils large and black. "There should have been four others. And my uncle. Where is my uncle?"

Waldo looked around. "He is not here, your highness."

"I can see that!" the king yowled. "Tell me something I don't know!"

Waldo twitched his whiskers twice, then shrugged. "I thought you knew everything, sire."

"Where. Is. My. Uncle?" King Griffen threw his crown to the floor, arched his back, got all puffed up, and threw a hissing fit. The three prisoners flinched while the guards stood unfazed.

"I do not know," Waldo said. "He never showed up."

"What do you mean he never showed up? I was told that..." The king stopped and looked at the prisoners, then regained his composure and retrieved his crown, placing it atop his undersized head before turning to Waldo. "Take the prisoners to the dungeon, then meet me in my chambers."

Waldo and his brothers bowed as the king stormed off and disappeared up the stairs.

"I think that went well," Neo whispered. "Don't you?"

Dino nodded. "Quite."

Waldo silenced them with a stare. "Let's go."

The three dogs and three cats marched away from the staircase through the cold and shadowed castle, along corridors and past guards at every corner, every door, every post. It appeared as though there were twenty guards for every one of them. By the time they reached the entrance to the dungeon, all six of the rebels questioned the wisdom of their actions.

As before, Finn, the flame point, guarded the dungeon door.

"Finn," Waldo said. "How's Fanny?"

"Fine," Finn said. "She's fine."

A fresh bandage on Finn's forehead marked Fanny's last furious fit.

Waldo favored Finn with a friendly forepaw. "Fanny's a fantastic feline."

Finn's eyelids fluttered, a nervous affliction effected by Fanny. "Are these the felons King Griffen forecasted?"

"Affirmative," Waldo said. "Four more to confine."

"Four?" Finn faltered for a few seconds. "I confront but

three."

"Unfortunate." Waldo furnished a fund of first-grade catnip and forced it upon Finn. One whiff and Finn fell face-first on the floor. As fate would follow, no feline foes confronted them.

"Is he out?" Fedora asked.

Neo checked him and nodded. "Like a bad dog."

"Good," Bogart said. "I don't think I could have endured any more alliteration."

"Do not knock names and nouns that share analogous nuances," Neo said. "You never know when you'll need them."

Dino nodded. "Don't deny your deepest desires. Dreams demand double devotion from distractions."

"That was good," Neo said.

Dino grinned. "Thank you."

"End your nonsense," Waldo said. "Time runs short."

Waldo grabbed the keys from Finn and opened the dungeon door while Neo dragged the unconscious flame point inside. The three canines followed, while Dino remained behind, taking Finn's post at the door.

"I must adjourn to the king's chambers," Waldo said, then licked one paw and groomed his face. "Is everyone clear on their responsibilities?"

Neo and the canines nodded.

"Good luck." Waldo passed the keys to Dino.

"Remember, await my signal."

Gwen licked Waldo once on the cheek. "May we meet again in freedom."

Waldo had never before been licked by a dog and found it odd that the dog's tongue was smooth rather than rough. But now was no time for whimsical pondering. He regarded Gwen and the others with a final nod before he turned and bounded down the hallway.

Behind him, Dino closed and locked the dungeon door, then passed the keys to Neo through the small, barred portal near the top of the door, their paws touching in brotherly affection.

"Don't be a hero," Neo said.

"What?" Dino said. "And let you have all the fun?"

Fedora tapped Neo on the shoulder. "We must go."

Neo nodded. "See you on the other side, brother."

"Not if I see you first," Dino said through the barred portal before he dropped from sight.

Taking one of the torches that lined the dungeon walls, Neo led Bogart, Gwen, and Fedora down the stairs, bypassing the first two levels. The canines could sense their friends in the cells, frightened and nervous, but they could not go to them yet. Their escape plan required calm and deliberation, emotions kept in check. But that was easier said in the toymaker's cottage than done in the dungeon while having to listen to the cries and whimpers of their forlorn canine comrades.

Fedora followed Neo, sniffing at the air, her ears up, while Gwen came closely behind her, seeking comfort. Bogart carried Finn, who had a satchel of catnip strapped to his face to keep him unconscious. Occasionally Finn's paws and whiskers twitched, but otherwise the flame point remained motionless.

When they reached the lowest level of the dungeon, the shadows that had hidden in the corners and cracks now spilled out like black paint. Not even Neo could see without the light from the torch, and even then only a few feet in front of him. A chilling dread emanated from the walls. The bewitching sense of calm Princess Eponine had felt upon entering the dungeon two days earlier had ceased to exist.

"Who's there?" Princess Eponine called out, for she could not see more than a couple of feet past the bars of her cell.

"It is I, Princess," Neo said as he approached.

"And who are you?" she asked, studying him in the faint light of the flickering torch he held.

Neo unlocked her cell door. "A friend of Prince Atticus and a loyal servant of Queen Lilith."

Princess Eponine walked out of her cell, where she saw a Saint Bernard, a border collie, and a golden retriever kneeling before her. "And who are they?"

"Your highness." Fedora raised her head. "We are

members of the rebellion, come to free you and the Maiden Poodle and restore the throne to Prince Atticus."

"My uncle?" the princess said. "Is he here?"

"He is on his way as we speak," Fedora said.

A soft whimper from another cell caught Fedora's attention. Behind her, Bogart and Gwen stared into the darkness and gasped, for around the cell the shadows appeared to move and pulse, almost as if alive. Against his better judgment, for it was poor etiquette to turn one's attention from a princess, Neo stared as well.

"Is that where...?" Bogart asked, his voice trailing off.

Princess Eponine nodded. "She is not well."

In the cell vacated by the princess, a single white rose stood bent over and dying, its leaves wilted and its white petals tinged with brown. One of the petals fell from the shrinking blossom and joined several other withered petals upon the stone floor.

As Neo walked over to the Maiden Poodle's cell and unlocked it, the others followed and stood in awe and fear, not knowing what to expect nor understanding what had happened. They could see nothing inside the cell but thick, shifting shadows.

"Why is it so dark?" Gwen asked.

"The darkness is feeding upon her," Princess Eponine said as she moved into the cell and crouched near a dark shape on the floor. When she stroked Camille, the Maiden

Poodle whined. Tears welled up in the princess's eyes. "She requires sunlight. If she does not get out of here soon, she will not survive."

"I was afraid of that," a voice said from behind them.

They all turned as Vincent, the white miniature poodle, walked past them and into the cell. In the darkness behind him appeared Prince Atticus along with Ian, who was dragging a heavy burlap sack.

"I feel a bit dog tired," Ian said, then smiled and gave a small bow. "Thank you. I'm here all week."

"Uncle!" Princess Eponine rushed from the cell and into the paws of Prince Atticus. "I feared I would never see you again."

"And I you," he said. "But we have no time for rejoicing. A dire situation is at hand."

"Dire indeed," Vincent said as he knelt over the Maiden Poodle who remained shrouded in shadows. "She has been in here too long. We must act now."

"It is too soon," Neo said. "We have to wait until Waldo..."

"There is no time to wait," Vincent said.

"Then act we will," Fedora said. The border collie turned to Bogart. "You are the only one strong enough to carry the Maiden Poodle. Are you up to it?"

The Saint Bernard, who was still carrying the unconscious Finn, deposited the flame point inside the other cell next to the dying rose and closed the door. Then he walked over to the Maiden Poodle and bent down, lifting Camille upon his back and shivering at the touch of the cold shadows that enveloped her, yet sensing something beneath the darkness: a warmth and calm such as he had never felt before. His heart swelled with resolve.

"I will not fail you," he whispered.

After the princess and Vincent helped secure the Maiden Poodle to Bogart's back with an old leash, Bogart carried Camille up the two flights to the dungeon door as Vincent and Ian hauled the burlap sack up behind him. Meanwhile, Neo led Fedora and Gwen to the cells on the other two levels, where they unlocked the doors and released the rebels along with the other prisoners. There were bulldogs and beagles, shelties and sheepdogs, pointers and pugs, mastiffs and mongrels—more than forty dogs and nearly as many breeds. All of them were excited to see Fedora and Gwen, wagging their tails and licking the faces of the golden retriever and the border collie. Occasionally, one of the prisoners would lick Neo, too.

"That is not necessary," Neo said, wiping at his cheek. "Really."

Once the prisoners were released, Fedora and Gwen took the keys and led the larger dogs who would not fit through the secret passage up the stairs to the dungeon door. The smaller dogs, twenty-five of them in all, followed

Neo back down to the lower level, where Prince Atticus and Princess Eponine awaited.

"Is everyone here?" Prince Atticus asked.

"All accounted for," Neo said.

"Then let us not waste any time." The red Persian took the lead and walked toward what appeared to be a solid wall.

"Where are we going?" asked a bedraggled Shih Tzu in desperate need of a grooming.

"To freedom," Prince Atticus said as he reached out and ticked a stone on the wall with a single claw. An instant later, a small opening appeared in the wall and the prince vanished inside.

Princess Eponine followed. The bedraggled Shih Tzu went next. One by one, the other prisoners disappeared into the opening that led from the dungeon into a secret passage that would take them through the bowels of the castle and beneath the moat to the exterior of the castle wall, where Stoker and Dresden awaited to lead them to a safe house.

Neo watched the last of the small canines enter the opening in the wall, then glanced up the stairs, wishing he could stay to help Waldo and Dino but knowing he was needed to help escort the rebels to safety once they reached the other side.

"Take care, my brothers," he whispered before he turned away from the stairs and followed the others into the secret passage.

He wondered if he would ever see them again.

Chapter 10

"Dino." Fedora stood on her hind legs with her paws against the dungeon door as she whispered through the barred portal. "Dino."

"Why does he not answer?" Bogart asked. The Maiden Poodle lay unconscious across his back, covered in shadows.

"I do not know," Fedora said. "Dino!"

Vincent ran a delicate paw across the Maiden Poodle's forehead as the shadows continued to swirl about her, expanding and contracting. "We need to get her outside."

The twenty other large canines released from the prison cells waited in silence, growing uneasy. A few began to whine.

"Dino," Fedora whispered again. "Dino!"

A moment later, Dino's face appeared on the other side of the small, barred portal. "What?"

"Where were you?" Fedora asked.

Dino smiled sheepishly. "I had to use the litter box."

"We are ready to go," Fedora said. She passed the keys to Dino. "Unlock the door."

Dino looked left and right along the corridor, his whiskers twitching. "But my brother Waldo has not returned."

"We cannot wait for him," Vincent said. "The Maiden Poodle grows weak. You must open the door now."

Dino glanced about nervously, his ears and whiskers twitching, then he dropped from sight. A moment later, the keys rattled in the lock and the door opened.

"I do not know if this is such a good idea," Dino said.

"We have no other choice," Vincent said.

Ian dragged the burlap sack over to the miniature white poodle.

"Are you sure this is going to work, laddie?" Ian asked.

Vincent nodded. "It has to. It's the only chance we have."

"Not exactly a ringing endorsement," Ian said. "But I guess it'll have to do."

Vincent turned to the group of canines who stood in the shadows behind him. "There are moments when you have to transcend who you are. When the past is a burden and the present is your only source of strength. When courage and character must rise up like a shield and a sword. This is such a moment. Do not let it pass."

With that, Vincent placed his paws on the burlap sack and closed his eyes. For several moments he remained that way, the canines and felines watching him in silence, not sure what he was doing. When Vincent opened his eyes and removed his paws from the sack, something inside the sack began to twitch.

"Everyone ready?" Vincent said.

The others nodded. When Vincent untied the sack and opened it, dozens of lizards and mice and birds raced out of the sack and along the corridor, spreading quickly throughout the castle.

Now some would call it cruel to stuff these small, harmless creatures into a burlap sack and drag them through a tunnel and then release them to their certain death in a castle filled with cats, but these were not ordinary lizards and mice and birds. These creatures were made of canvas and felt, yarn and thread, stitched together by the toymaker Popo Santiago and filled with catnip.

Under normal conditions, these toys would not move of their own accord, for they were, after all, only toys. But as the Maiden Poodle had demonstrated to Princess Eponine when she had called the white rose from stone, the energy of life is not restricted by boundaries, but flows in a continuous cycle. And as such, the toys were not truly alive but rather called to life by Vincent, as they were imbued with the life force transferred to them by the paws of the toymaker.

"How long will this last?" Fedora asked as the toys disappeared down the corridor.

"Our window of opportunity is small," Vincent said. He glanced at the Maiden Poodle, her motionless body shrouded in a cocoon of shadows. "The darkness in this place saps my powers as we speak. This diversion will not last long."

"Then let us not delay," Bogart said. The Saint Bernard stepped into the corridor and nodded to Dino. "Lead the way."

With a nervous meow, Dino took the lead. Bogart, Gwen, and Vincent followed, while the twenty rebel prisoners fell in behind them. Ian moved to bring up the rear until Fedora stopped him. "You must go and join the others at the safe house," she said.

"Excuse me, lassie," he said. "But I believe my services are needed here."

"Your services are needed with the others," Fedora said. "You are small enough to fit through the secret passage. Bogart and Gwen and I are not. If we do not succeed in our escape, the rebellion will need your leadership."

"Lassie, I do not think..."

"There is no time for discussion. You must go." Fedora turned and ran down the corridor after the others.

"But I..." Ian said.

And then the border collie was gone, leaving Ian alone in the corridor, wondering what action to take. The sound of approaching paws made the decision for him, hastening the Scottie back into the dungeon.

He shut the door and stood back in the shadows, his heart pounding as the sound of paws approached, claws clicking rapidly on stone. Then they passed and continued down the corridor until the only noise was the sound of Ian's own panting.

With his nose, Ian nudged open the door and peeked into the corridor. For several moments he considered leaving the dungeon and following after the others to aid them in their escape, but Fedora had told him to join the others and he did not want to disrespect her wishes. After all, nothing is worse than a disobedient dog.

And there was something else. Something Fedora had said. Something Ian could not ignore.

The rebellion will need your leadership.

Ian had never thought of himself as a leader, as someone to whom others would look for courage and direction. But Fedora must have seen something in Ian that he was not aware of, a quality he thought he had been lacking, and he did not intend to disappoint her. He would join the others at the safe house and show them the leadership Fedora had seen.

As Ian closed the door and descended the stairs, he recalled what Vincent had said about courage and character, about transcending who you were, and pride filled him up like a balloon. But as every dog knows, an inflated sense of pride can often lead to an unforeseen fall.

Ian raced down the stairs, his mind preoccupied as he envisioned himself walking through the streets of Felinia, signing autographs and kissing puppies, greeted by his canine comrades with admiration and devotion. In the thickening shadows of the stairwell, he did not see the loose stone that awaited him.

One of Ian's hind paws hit the stone and he lost his footing. In the eagerness of his descent he fell forward, landing awkwardly on his forelegs. Something snapped and Ian let out a yelp as he tumbled down the stairs to the lowest level, landing in a panting heap on the cold stones. Pain and panic shot through him. He attempted to stand, but his left foreleg was broken and his rear hip on the opposite side burned like a blacksmith's iron. He could not stand up.

For an instant Ian almost cried out for help, until he realized if anyone were to hear him it would most likely be one of King Griffen's guards rather than one of his canine comrades.

Ian looked up and saw the opening to the secret passage not ten feet away. Using his right foreleg and left hind leg,

Ian attempted to crawl across the floor to the passage, whimpering as the pain from his injuries overwhelmed him, dulling his senses. Shadows crept up at the edges of his vision.

He glanced once more at the opening to the secret passage, despairing at his inability to reach it, to close it and preserve the escape of his friends. Then Ian's eyes fluttered shut and he fell unconscious as the shadows of the dungeon swirled around him.

Chapter II

Throughout the castle, King Griffen's guards abandoned their posts and raced through the corridors, their excited meows and yowls echoing off the stone walls. Bogart and Vincent stood strong, as did Fedora and Gwen and most of the escaped canines, though some of the rebels were terrified, and I don't have to tell you how sad it is to see a grown Doberman whimper. Yet the rebels were not in immediate danger, for the cries and yowls from the cats were directed not at the escaping canines but at the catnip-filled creatures that scurried and flew about the castle.

As the two-dozen dogs and Dino hastened along the corridors, cats raced past them preoccupied—spears and swords and shields discarded as they chased after mice and lizards or leapt at birds. Some of the guards who caught one of the toys would play with them, bat at them, let them go, and then pounce on them again. Others would catch the toys and roll around on the castle floor, stretching out and looking silly, while others, like Finn, fell asleep.

"I would not have believed this had I not seen it with my own eyes," Gwen whispered to Bogart.

The Saint Bernard said nothing, his eyes and ears alert, sensing that the present ease of their escape would soon come to an end. On his back, the Maiden Poodle twitched as if from a bad dream.

Vincent glanced once at Camille, at the darkness that continued to feed upon her, and urged Dino to quicken his pace. The others followed suit, avoiding the playful batting of a grinning calico and skirting past a pair of snoring Siamese as the rebels continued their journey toward the castle's main gate.

Meanwhile, outside the castle, across the moat and near a hidden opening at the west gate, Stoker and Dresden waited in the pre-dawn darkness for the emergence of Prince Atticus and Princess Eponine and the group of smaller canine rebels.

"Where are they?" Stoker whined.

"They are coming," Dresden said. The greyhound sat relaxed but alert. "Have patience, my friend."

"But shouldn't they have been here by now?" Stoker asked. He looked around, nervous. Not only did all of this waiting make him anxious, but he was also afraid of the dark.

"They will be here when they will be here," Dresden said.

"What is that supposed to mean?"

"It means that plans are at the mercy of fate, so it serves no purpose to worry," Dresden said. "You worry a good deal."

"I know. I can't help it."

Dresden nodded, then gave the beagle a smile. "Perhaps it serves a purpose."

Before Stoker could ask Dresden what purpose his worrying served, several figures appeared out of the darkness across from them.

"They have arrived," Dresden said.

The two dogs watched in vigilant silence as Prince Atticus led Princess Eponine and the twenty-five prisoners from the hidden passage, with Neo bringing up the rear.

"Did it go well?" Stoker asked.

"The Maiden Poodle's health is in question," Prince Atticus said, "which forced the others to move earlier than planned."

"But you are all accounted for?" Dresden asked.

The prince nodded.

"Then we must escort you to safety," the greyhound said.

As Dresden began to lead the band of rebels away from the castle, Stoker looked around. "Where is Ian?"

"He stayed behind to help with the toys," Neo said.

Stoker glanced back at the bushes that covered the tunnel. "Shouldn't we wait for him?"

"We do not have time," Dresden said. "If the others fail in their attempt at escape, the guards will be searching for us. If we are to help our comrades, we cannot afford to be caught."

"But I am..."

Stoker left the last word unspoken, for he did not want the others to think poorly of him, but he could not help worrying.

Dresden studied the beagle a moment and nodded. "Wait if you must. But if Ian has not arrived within five minutes, you must find your way discreetly to the safe house."

From his position across from the west gate, Stoker watched the twenty-five canines and three felines disappear into the early morning darkness and around a corner, then he turned his attention to the spot in the bushes where Prince Atticus had emerged moments before. He waited, hoping and worrying, each minute that passed raising his anxiety until it was all he could do to keep from howling.

When the fifth minute passed, Stoker let out a soft whine, then turned to follow the others in the direction of the safe house.

Back in the castle, as the guards played with the catnip toys and the rebels made their way toward the main gate, Waldo sat silent in the king's royal chambers while King Griffen stormed about the room and yelled at him.

"Is it asking too much, is it really so hard, to grasp what is expected of you as a guard?"

The king hissed and yowled as he paced north and south, flecks of foam and saliva flying out of his mouth.

"All I asked you to do was arrest seven dogs, no more and no less, is your head in a fog? You brought back but three, four less than I needed. It's as if my instructions went completely unheeded."

While the king could put up with some occasional lapses, Waldo's brain, he believed, lacked the proper synapses.

"I also requested one cat, my dear uncle, but even that order you managed to bungle." The king glared at Waldo, his eyes full and black, then he took two steps forward as if to attack.

"Now listen up close, I don't want you to miss a single

word that I say," he said with a hiss. "You've used up your credits, received your last break, for tonight you have made your final mistake."

The king gave a smile, then strolled 'cross the floor, his tail twitching twice as he opened the door.

"Come sunrise, which occurs in less than an hour, you will behold how a king wields the weight of his power. Guards!" he called out and into his room came two cats, both black, named Danger and Doom.

"Take him to the tower, along with his brothers. And when that is done," said the king, "seize their mother."

The two guards took Waldo, who said not a word, but instead for some reason he quietly purred. The king closed the door and returned to his bed, then he looked about, puzzled, with his undersized head.

"I don't understand why it seems every time that while in my chambers the prose comes in rhyme."

As the king scratched his ear and sat down to ponder, into the room, on its own, a toy mouse did wander. His eyes growing large, King Griffen crouched low and crawled to the edge of his bed, soft and slow. With a twitch of his tail he got ready to jump, then he pounced from the bed to the floor with a *thump*.

What events followed next I don't wish to relate for they might have a bearing on this fairy tale's fate. So we take leave of the king and the catnip-filled toy to discover if

Waldo found sorrow or joy. His comrades, on Waldo, their fortunes depend. Now the verse, and this chapter, have come to an end.

Chapter 12

It is well known that a canine of virtually every breed, or mix of breeds, will chase a ball or a stick or a flying disc for hours on end, unable to quell the urge to fetch regardless of how exhausted he or she becomes. Some experts, mostly feline in nature, maintain that the reason for this canine behavior stems from a missing biological switch that governs rational thought, in addition to a general lack of self-control.

Other experts, mostly canines, contend that dogs just want to have fun.

Cats, on the other hand, do not play for hour after hour with a single toy, or anything else for that matter. They soon lose interest and move on to another activity, such as grooming or eating or getting some beauty rest. Feline experts point to the cat's impressive intellect and healthy self-esteem for a desire to pursue diverse interests. Certain canine experts, however, believe that the cat's inability to maintain interest in elementary games is due to a short attention span, an idle lifestyle, and an unparalleled obsession with cleanliness.

In any event, it is well known that cats tend to lose interest with toys after a fashion, catnip and magical enchantments notwithstanding. So even before Vincent's powers dissipated and the mice and lizards and birds became nothing but inert toys made of cloth and catnip, many of the guards had stopped playing and returned to their posts with their customary dignified expressions that belied the foolishness in which they had just partaken. By the time the rebels reached the portcullis that led through the main gate and out to the drawbridge, three of the six guards positioned at the gate had returned, armed and attentive.

"Greetings," the head guard said, a rare Norwegian forest cat named Bob.

Dino gulped once, then he squeaked out an identical response. Without his brother, Waldo, there to offer support, Dino lacked self-confidence and knew not what to do.

Bob studied the group of canines who stood nervous and silent, their eyes filled with both hope and fear. "Are these not the prisoners who are set to stand trial today?"

"No," Dino said. "I mean yes. Yes they are."

The other two guards, both twenty-pound tomcats, looked on with feline indifference.

"Why are they not in their cells?" Bob asked.

"I'm...I'm," stammered Dino, trying to come up with a reason until one finally came to him. "I'm taking them for a walk."

At the mention of the word *walk*, all of the canines began wagging their tails, while several of them cocked their heads.

Bob eyed the rebels with suspicion, then returned his attention to Dino. "I was not informed of this."

Behind Dino, Vincent ran a concerned paw across the Maiden Poodle, her form all but obscured by the cocoon of shadows. Outside, the stars began to fade as the first light of morning approached.

"We must get her outside," Vincent said.

Bob looked at the white miniature poodle, incredulous. "What did he say?"

Dino's expression grew bewildered as he struggled for something to say, his mouth opening and closing like a fish fighting for air.

"I...he..."

"You heard what he said," a voice said from upon the stairs. Everyone turned as Waldo came bounding down the spiral staircase to the stone floor.

At the sight of his brother, Dino experienced a relief so great that it was sensed by several characters in another fairy tale.

Behind Waldo came the two black cats, Danger and Doom. Unbeknownst to King Griffen, Danger and Doom shared sympathies with the rebellion and wished to help restore the throne to Prince Atticus. They resented their roles as King Griffen's bodyguards and the threatening connotation of their identities, which, needless to say, created difficulties when it came to dating and making friends.

"What know you of this matter?" Bob asked.

"I know the king's wishes," Waldo said. "And he wishes for his prisoners to be in good health when he hands down his judgment."

Bob glanced at the band of rebels. "They appear healthy enough."

"This one is rather ill." Waldo motioned toward the Maiden Poodle. "She requires sunlight and fresh air to improve her condition. The king specifically requested that she be allowed a few minutes outside."

Bob studied the shifting shadows that surrounded Camille, then he pointed a single claw at the other rebel canines. "What of these others?"

"It is their final request." Waldo glanced at his brother. "They are in need of a walk."

The rebels' tails once more wagged in unison. Several of the dogs looked at Waldo eagerly and started panting.

"This is not standard procedure," Bob said. "I require the king's official..."

"There is no time for discussion!" Waldo pointed once more to the Maiden Poodle. "Can you not see that she is ill? That she may not make it to see her own execution? I would not wish to be the one to have to tell King Griffen the name of the guard who allowed his prisoner to avoid royal judgment."

Bob licked his paw and cleaned distractedly behind one ear. Then he looked at the two other guards, neither of whom wanted any part of the responsibility that had befallen him.

"By the way," Waldo said. "What is your name again?"

Wearing an expression of resignation, Bob approached the large wheel that operated the portcullis and turned the gears until the barrier had been raised to its full height, then he started to crank the wheel that lowered the drawbridge. A few minutes later, the rebels began to make their slow and deliberate escape from the castle.

As Waldo and Dino led the rebels through the gate and out into the cool morning air, Danger and Doom brought up the rear. Across the drawbridge, a large rolling meadow separated the castle from the village, a vision of freedom, and it appeared as if the rebels would reach safety unchallenged. But as is often the case, both in fairy tales and in other worlds, appearances can be deceiving.

At the same time that Dino and the rebels reached the main gate and encountered Bob the Norwegian forest cat, a tailless orange Manx by the name of Max and a gray tabby named Sam stood outside the dungeon entrance, pondering what had happened to the flame point named Finn.

"Taking a catnap," Max said.

"Playing a fiddle," Sam said.

"On a hot tin roof," Max said.

While pondering further, they found that the door to the dungeon was unlocked and, upon entering the dungeon and descending the stairs, discovered that the cells on the top two levels were empty of prisoners.

"This is bad," Max said.

"Unfavorable," Sam agreed.

"Inauspicious," Max said.

While Sam went to alert the king of the prisoners' escape, Max continued to investigate the top two floors of the dungeon, checking all of the cells and wishing he had a tail to swish back and forth like Sam and the other guards. He often dreamt he had a long, fluffy tail that rose out behind him like a royal plume.

As Max continued to fantasize about his imaginary tail, Ian awoke and lay panting on the cold dungeon floor one level below, the pain in his foreleg and hip a reminder of his tumble down the stairs. But he had no time for pity.

The Scottie dragged himself across the floor, fighting against the urge to whine or yelp as the darkness and shadows threatened to close in on him and ferry him once more into unconsciousness. He did not know if he could make it into the secret passage before he passed out, but he had to close the door to the passage so he could buy his friends some time to escape.

Above him, Ian heard the sound of claws on stone, paws approaching the top of the stairs, and he knew his time was almost out. He scooted across the floor toward the secret passage, reaching for the hidden switch, desperation driving him forward, only to collapse short of his goal as darkness and despair washed over him.

"I am sorry," Ian said, his voice nothing more than a whisper.

A moment later, someone reached out and grabbed him.

"I've got you," the voice said.

Max the Manx was just descending the stairs to the bottom level when he heard a yelp and a whine below him, along with scuffling and the sound of claws scratching against stone. With his sword drawn and his shield held out in front of him, Max continued down the stairs, his ears turning and his nose twitching, his fur standing up and a low growl emanating from his throat.

When he reached the lower level, Max peered into the shadows that danced at the edges of the faint light given off by a flickering wall torch, but he saw nothing, neither dog nor cat. Not even a rat. Behind him, Max thought he heard another whine, but when he turned to look, all he found was a solid wall of stone.

A quick search of the six cells on the lower level revealed no signs of any canine prisoners, although Max did find the answer to one of the questions he and Sam had pondered.

He had been right. Finn was, indeed, taking a catnap.

In the darkness of the secret passage, Ian let out a soft whine, followed by a whispered admonition. "Easy, laddie. That leg's broken."

"Sorry," Stoker whispered as he helped his friend through the passage.

After he had turned to follow Dresden and the others to the safe house as instructed, Stoker had taken no more than a half dozen steps before his growing anxiety about Ian had compelled him to return to the west gate and approach the bushes protecting the passage. Hesitation had preceded his decision to enter, for the passage was dark and Stoker was no hero, his canine attributes lacking a streak of courage. But he possessed a big heart and a faithful sense of friendship. And that was all he needed.

Without any light and without the eyes of a cat to help him see, Stoker slowly made his way through the dark confines of the passage, trying his best not to injure his friend. Or himself.

"Ow," Stoker said as he bumped his head. "I cannot see where I am going."

"Aye," Ian said. "But it's a good deal better than seeing your way into a locked cell. Or the executioner's noose."

In the darkness Stoker smiled, for although he had not asked for nor expected a *thank you* from Ian, he understood that, in his own way, the Scottie had offered just that.

For what felt like hours but took less time than a flea bath, Stoker and Ian inched their way through the passage until, before they realized it, they were able to see one another. And indeed there was faint light, filtering into the passage through the bushes that masked the entrance.

When Stoker and Ian finally emerged from the passage, the sun had not yet risen above the mountains. But the lord of night had given way to the empress of dawn, and the village and the kingdom waited beneath the azure sky that unfurled across the heavens, as if all of Felinia sensed what was to come.

Chapter 13

In the chill of the burgeoning dawn, four cats and two-dozen rebel canines hurried across the drawbridge, their breath blowing out in smoky plumes, the castle rising up dark and foreboding behind them. Less than two minutes away, the green rolling meadow beckoned to them with a whisper of freedom that grew louder as they drew near.

Upon Bogart's sturdy back, the shadows coalesced around the Maiden Poodle, eagerly feeding, sucking the life force from her, for that is what the darkness does. It feeds. And when it feeds, it grows stronger and more powerful until it consumes everything that is good.

Halfway to the meadow, the canine rebels all stopped a moment and cocked their heads in unison, sensing danger, as dogs are known to do. After several moments they continued unchallenged, hoping perhaps that their senses had betrayed them. But an instant later an alarm wailed, the yowl of a hundred cats in unison. Within seconds, dozens of guards appeared on the castle walls and dozens more raced through the main gate onto the drawbridge.

"Run!" Fedora shouted.

And run they did. With their size and speed, the canines easily outpaced the cats and reached the other side of the moat, where they dashed out into the open meadow—all except Bogart who, with the weight and responsibility of the Maiden Poodle upon his back, could not keep up with the others.

Seeing this, Vincent fell back with the Saint Bernard, as did Gwen and Fedora, who herded the others as best she could while the escaped prisoners scattered across the meadow. Waldo and Dino remained behind as well, but even with the help of Danger and Doom, the four felines would be no match to defend the Maiden Poodle against King Griffen and his guards.

"They are gaining on us," Dino said, glancing over his shoulder as they hurried across the meadow.

"We can make it," Fedora panted. "We have to make it!"

But as they reached a rise of the rolling meadow, Fedora's hopeful proclamations fell silent. Awaiting her and the others were nearly four-dozen of the king's guards who had been patrolling the village and had responded to the alarm. Already they had managed to capture nearly half of the escaped prisoners, surrounding them with drawn swords, hissing and puffing themselves up and bounding sideways at the dogs, many of whom whined and cowered at the display; for while the canines were bigger, the felines were more ferocious. And even the largest and most courageous of dogs backed down when swatted across the nose by one of the king's guards.

Before Fedora and the others could help their comrades or flee, the castle guards closed in from behind and surrounded them, cutting off all routes of escape.

Moments later, above the mountains that ringed the kingdom, the first glimpse of the sun appeared.

"Lay down your weapons!" said the captain of the guards, a Himalayan named Horatio, who pointed his sword at Waldo, Dino, Danger, and Doom.

Outnumbered and surrounded, with no way out that would not result in numerous casualties, the four rebel felines relinquished their spears and shields.

"Seize them!" Horatio the Himalayan commanded.

Within seconds, Waldo, Dino, Danger, and Doom were pounced upon by their former feline comrades, their forepaws shackled behind them. Gwen, Fedora, Vincent and Bogart—the Maiden Poodle still resting motionless upon his back—stood huddled together on the meadow, surrounded by fangs and claws, drawn swords and spears. They did not look at one another, for they did not wish to see their despair mirrored in one another's eyes.

Dreams are not easily attained and wishes do not always come true. But when a hope that has been envisioned is within reach, when it is close enough to touch and feel before it is yanked away at the last second, no one can understand such a moment unless it has been experienced.

Such was the anguish of the rebel canines.

As the sun slowly continued to rise, a flourish of trumpets and the parting of feline bodies heralded the arrival of King Griffen, who paraded around like a proud peacock, his jeweled crown catching a glint from the sliver of sun that had crept above the mountains.

Now some may think that the rebels' undoing was due to the dark effects of the castle that had diluted Vincent's powers and caused the catnip-filled toys to fall inert. Others will argue that the discovery of the empty dungeon by Sam and Max was what led to the foiled escape. But while these factors played a part, the catalyst was none other than the king himself. For at the moment when King Griffen had pounced from his bed to the floor to attack the toy catnip mouse, he was stopped by the memory of the dream in which just such a pursuit had resulted in the appearance of a dragon-sized mouse. Sensing something amiss, the king pondered the catnip mouse for several minutes before he left his chambers and descended the stairs, arriving at the main gate to discover the drawbridge lowered and the rebels escaping. Bob, the rare Norwegian forest cat who had allowed the prisoners to leave, had earned himself his own private cell in the dungeon.

King Griffen strutted about the meadow, stopping in front of Waldo and his rebellious cohorts. "Your lack of loyalty disappoints me," the king said, glaring at Danger and Doom. "The punishment you receive will be worse than you can imagine and will serve as an example to those who would dare defy the throne."

"We do not defy the throne," Waldo said. "We defend it of its rightful heir."

"I am its rightful heir!" King Griffen hissed. "And you shall soon know the consequences of your traitorous actions."

He glared at the four felines a moment longer before he turned his pitiless gaze upon the rebel canines who stood defiant but subdued, resigned to their fate. The king smiled at them, a smile with more fangs than mirth, and swept a forepaw across the landscape from the village to the castle and the mountains beyond.

"This is my kingdom," King Griffen said. "Everything in it belongs to me to do with as I please. I find it amusing that you would think otherwise. I shall show you and the inhabitants of Felinia the folly of your resistance and how I deal with those who defy their king."

Gwen shivered and whined while Bogart and Vincent stood defiant. Fedora stared at King Griffen, unblinking, her expression a stoic mask that hid her fear and disappointment.

King Griffen glanced about the meadow, observing the canine prisoners, most of whom had been captured, then turned back to Fedora and the others. "I do not see my sister. Nor do I see nearly half of the other traitors who resided in my dungeon. Where are they? Tell me now or you will experience suffering such as you have never known."

Gwen, Fedora, Bogart, and Vincent regarded the king with unwavering silence.

The king stepped closer. "Let me make myself clear. If you do not willingly inform me of their whereabouts, I will be forced to extract the information from you in other ways. And when you do finally break, you will bear witness to the punishment I mete out on those who escaped and those who helped them. You will watch your friends perish."

While the rebels knew the king did not make idle threats, they stood strong and defiant, willing to remain silent and risk their own pain and suffering for their comrades.

"Very well, then," King Griffen said. "You leave me no choice."

Above the mountains, the sun continued to rise, peeking

over the rocks and trees, its brilliant light falling upon the castle, slowly working its way down to the drawbridge and across the moat.

King Griffen flashed a false smile, then turned his merciless gaze upon the Maiden Poodle's shadow-shrouded form secured to Bogart's back.

"Untie her!" the king said.

A pair of Siamese cats approached Bogart, who bared his teeth and growled until Fedora and Vincent calmed him. Once the two cats loosened the leash, Vincent and Fedora lowered the Maiden Poodle to the dew-covered meadow, where she lay on her side, unconscious and barely breathing as the shadows shifted and twitched around her.

"I have heard that some of you believe this dog, this poodle, is some kind of sorceress," the king said. "A wizard of sorts. Is that true?"

Once again, silence answered him.

"It is of no matter," King Griffen said. "For whether she is or is not, she will be nothing soon enough. You!" He pointed to a silver-spotted tabby who stood guarding the four rebel canines. "Strike her down."

"No!" Fedora barked as she moved forward to intercede, only to be blocked by spears and swords from several of the king's guards.

"Tell me where my sister is," King Griffen said, "and I will reconsider."

Fedora turned to look at Vincent, who shook his head. Then she looked once more at the Maiden Poodle before she lowered her eyes to the ground.

"Foolish dogs," King Griffen said. He pointed once more at the motionless form of the Maiden Poodle. "Strike her down!"

The silver tabby approached the Maiden Poodle and raised his spear as if to strike, but a flicker of something deep within his conscience stopped him. He had never sensed such a thing before and could not describe it later if asked to do so, but at that moment he understood that he could not heed the king's orders.

The light from the sunrise continued to creep across the drawbridge and had now reached the edge of the meadow.

"I command you to strike her down," King Griffen yowled.

Instead of obeying, the tabby lowered his spear and stepped back, not knowing for certain why he had stopped, only understanding that he could not bring harm to the defenseless creature that lay before him.

King Griffen stormed over to the guard and swiped the spear from his paws. "It is obvious to see why some of us are king and others are not."

Turning from the guard, King Griffen stepped toward the Maiden Poodle and raised the spear above his head. For just an instant the king, too, hesitated, a shadow of doubt flickering through his undersized head, which he shook in an attempt to rid himself of the unfamiliar thoughts.

Sensing an opportunity, Bogart broke away from the cats guarding him and lunged at King Griffen in an effort to wrest the spear from him, but the king's cat-like reflexes were too fast. In a flash, King Griffen ducked, avoiding Bogart's powerful forepaws, and plunged his spear into the Saint Bernard's side.

"No!" Gwen cried.

Bogart collapsed to the meadow in a heap, his side rising and falling, the handle of the spear pointing straight up toward the sky. Fedora cried out to him along with Gwen, but Bogart did not hear them. His thoughts were not of the pain that engulfed him, nor of the life flowing from his wound, but of the promise to the Maiden Poodle that he had failed to keep.

At that very moment, a shaft of light from the rising sun worked its way across the meadow and reached the Maiden Poodle. Beneath the skin of dark shadows that stretched across her, a faint glow appeared, white and unearthly. King Griffen, standing closest to her, stepped away in fear, uncertain of what was taking place. The king's guards backed away as well, though not in fear but in awe, their eyes wide and tails twitching.

The light inside the cocoon of darkness that enshrouded the Maiden Poodle continued to glow brighter and brighter until the cocoon finally split open, the darkness falling away from Camille and on to the meadow like oil, absorbing into the ground. And then it was gone.

With a yawn, Camille stood up and stretched in the invigorating sunshine, turning her head this way and that, her eyes falling upon all of those around her. Vincent smiled with delight, as did Fedora and Gwen, though their smiles soon turned to frowns of concern as the Maiden Poodle approached Bogart, who lay on his side panting, his eyes half closed. A series of soft whimpers escaped him.

The Maiden Poodle leaned down toward Bogart and whispered in his ear. "You did not fail me."

Camille closed her eyes and placed her paws on Bogart. An instant later, the spear began to glow, burning bright like the core of a flame. Before anyone could react to what was happening, the spear turned into white smoke that vanished inside Bogart as if sucked into the wound. The Saint Bernard opened his eyes wide and gasped. The next moment, black smoke erupted from the wound, shooting up into the air and turning into dozens of blackbirds, dark as night, which swirled about in a single cloud above the meadow and then flew off.

At that point, many of the guards turned and fled for the safety of the castle, while others dropped their spears and swords and stared in wonder at Bogart, who was no longer on his side but standing on all four paws, his tail wagging. The wound from the spear was gone.

As Fedora and Gwen rushed up to Bogart, unchecked by the fleeing guards, King Griffen recognized that control of the situation was abandoning him. Still, this was his kingdom, and he remained King Griffen the Great. His title demanded respect.

"Seize them!" he yowled as he stormed across the meadow, exhorting his guards. "I command you to seize them!"

But none of the guards picked up their arms or made any move toward the rebels, for all had witnessed the Maiden Poodle's powers and glimpsed a truth previously unknown to them, an understanding of their existence that could not be ignored.

The king understood this as well, but he did not accept it. He could not accept it because it meant he was not in charge and he could not let it be so.

Frustrated and desperate, King Griffen picked up a spear and turned toward the Maiden Poodle. Before he could take another step, the sound of beating wings filled the air. As everyone turned to watch, the cloud of blackbirds returned and descended upon King Griffen, knocking the spear from his claws and lifting him up into the air, carrying him from the meadow, beyond the castle, until birds and cat vanished into the blue morning sky.

Chapter 14

During the days that followed, there was much rejoicing throughout Felinia. The charges of illegitimacy against Prince Atticus were found untruthful and dismissed, allowing him to return to the castle and take his proper place upon the throne. Thus began the reign of King Atticus the Noble.

Waldo, Dino, and Neo were knighted by the new king and made his official royal advisers, while Princess Eponine joined her uncle in ruling the land in what would eventually become a golden age for Felinia: a time when dogs and cats worked together in peace and harmony for the common good of the kingdom.

The land that King Griffen had taken from the canine farmers was returned to them in full, with the barons offering their former servants a year's supply of gourmet dog biscuits and high-grade kibble for their troubles. In turn, the farmers grew organic catnip for their feline neighbors. The demand for catnip-filled toys and birds and lizards became so great that Popo Santiago became Felinia's official toymaker. So popular did his toys become that he opened a store in the Maiden Poodle's home of Watonia, where he resides to this day.

Ian's injured leg and hip were healed by the Maiden Poodle, though the Scottie still occasionally walked with a limp to get sympathy and attention. Ian, Bogart, Gwen, Fedora, Dresden, and Stoker were all given Medals of Honor for their bravery and service to the kingdom before they all returned to their lives as normal citizens—although they still received the occasional request for an autograph. Meanwhile, Yancy, the shepherd-wolf mix, was banished to The Valley of Despair, where he opened a shelter for runaway half-breeds.

The Maiden Poodle remained in Felinia through the end of the summer, making several appearances as a motivational speaker before she returned to her homeland with Vincent, where she and others like her used their powers to help those less fortunate in other lands.

The darkness that absorbed into the meadow reappeared a short time later, sprouting from the ground as dark, thorny weeds that soon produced bright crimson flowers. These flowers gave off an intoxicating scent before they died off, leaving a cluster of black seeds that were taken by the first wind of autumn and spread far and wide. For as the Maiden Poodle and her ancestors were well aware, the darkness could never be vanquished, but only held at bay. It would continue to search for shadows in which to grow, both in dark and desolate lands and in the hearts and minds of those who let it in.

As for King Griffen, who was no longer the ruler of Felinia (or of any land for that matter), the cloud of blackbirds carried him beyond The Valley of Despair, beyond the kingdom of Felinia, beyond The Great Sea, to another island where every twelfth mouse grew as large as a dragon and cats were required to work long hours in sweatshops making cheese for a pittance.

But that is another story.

About the Author

S.G. Browne is the author of the novels *Less Than Hero*, *Big Egos*, *Lucky Bastard*, *Fated*, and *Breathers*, as well as the eBook short story collection *Shooting Monkeys in a Barrel* and the heartwarming holiday tale *I Saw Zombies Eating Santa Claus*. When he's not writing, he reads books, watches movies, practices tai chi, and volunteers at the SPCA, where he adopted a seven-year-old calico tabby named Marlo. You can learn more about his books and his writing at www.sgbrowne.com.

Made in the USA
Lexington, KY
14 July 2017